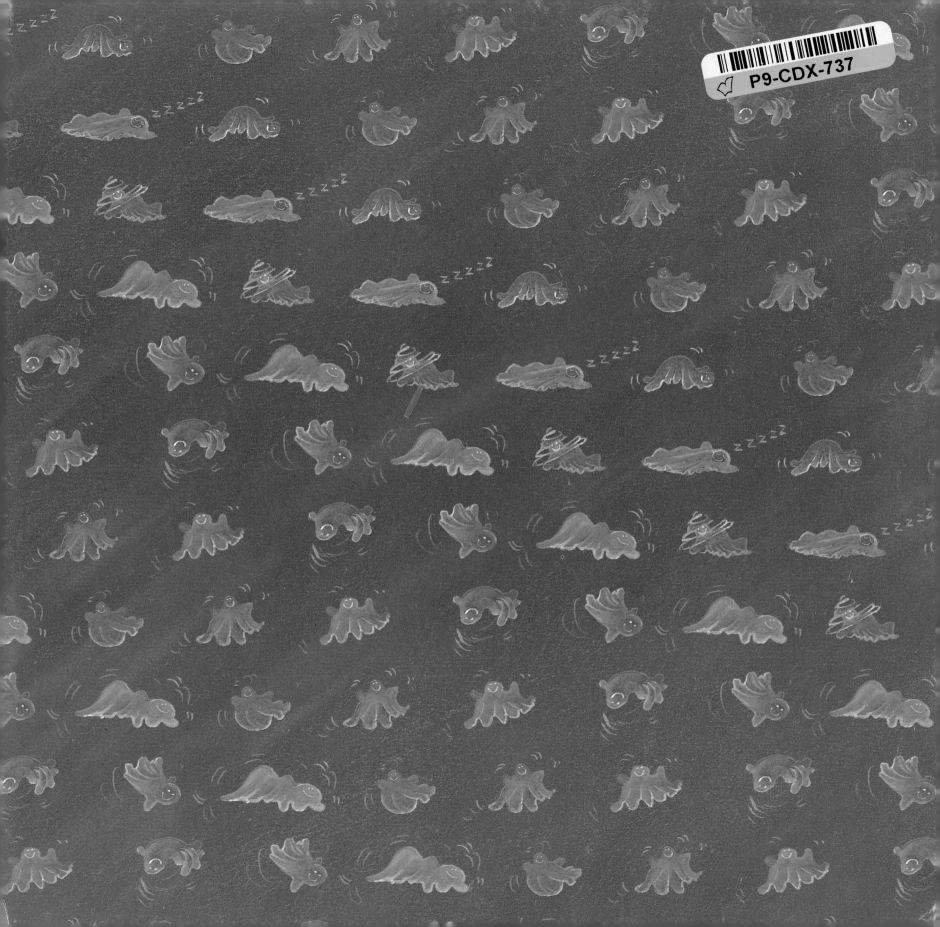

This book is dedicated to
my cat, Catsi, (1982 – 1996).
He is now what he
always wanted
to be...
a
Rottweiler!

DROP DEAD

Babette Cole

Alfred A. Knopf 🐎 New York

"Gran and Granddad, why are you such bald old wrinklies?"

"We were bald wrinkly babies once!"

"We learned dribbling and burping . . .

potty training,

and how to say simple words like
poo-poo and pee-pee.

Poo Poo
and
Pee Pee

We learned crawling,

standing on one leg,

running and jumping!

Then we went to school.

As we grew older, we played different games.

At six years old.

At ten years old.

At sixteen years old.

When we were teenagers,
we experimented with . . .

smoking . . .

driving Dad's car . . .

falling in love with
the wrong person,

falling in love with
the right person

and not being
approved of.

We continued our
experiments at college!

We had college parties.

We failed to get jobs as scientists!
So we went to work in films.

Granddad became   a stuntman!

Grandma became a famous film star!

We fell in love and got married . . .

. . . on location!

We had your father—this was the only way
we could get him to bed.

When he grew up, he became a famous
crocodile wrestler on the Nile.

There he met your mother

and they had you.

When we became grandparents, we retired,

and as we grew older,
we became more
wrinkly.

We've got false teeth!

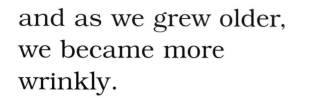

Granddad has gone quite bald!

We forget things!

We've shrunk a bit . . .

but we still try the
odd stunt.

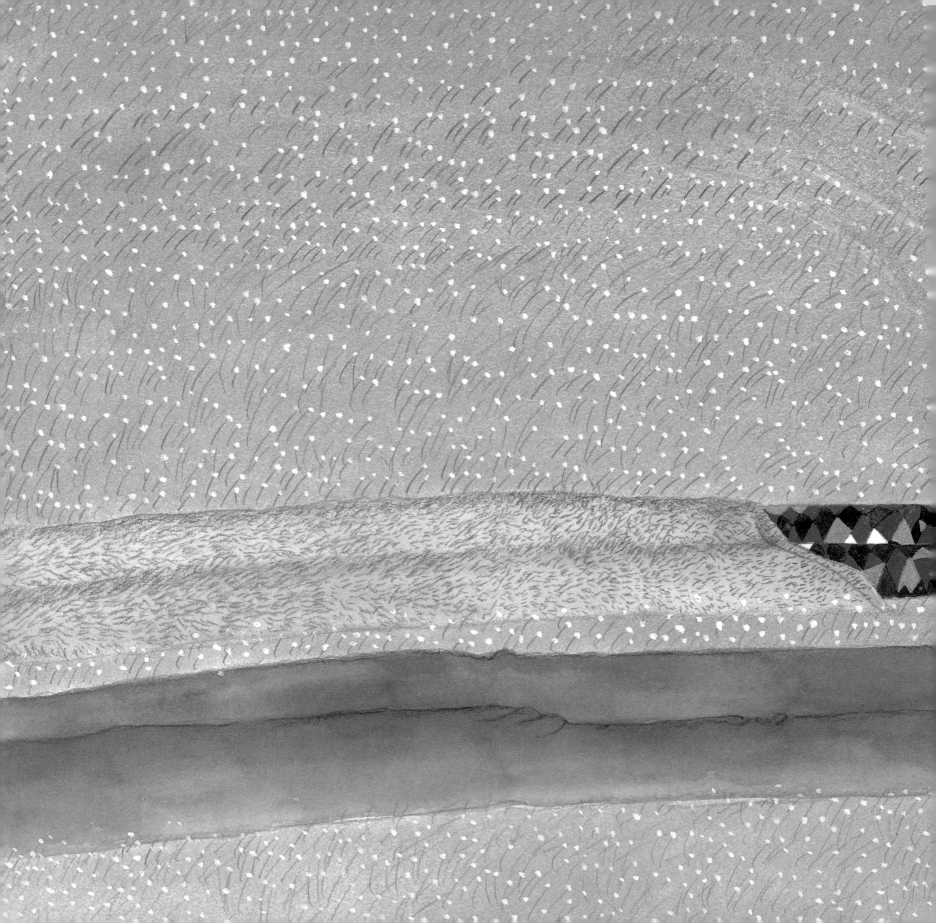

Even though we've led such dangerous lives, one day we'll just drop down dead like everyone else.

Then we might be recycled
as anything at all!

An octopus

a moose

a new baby

a worm

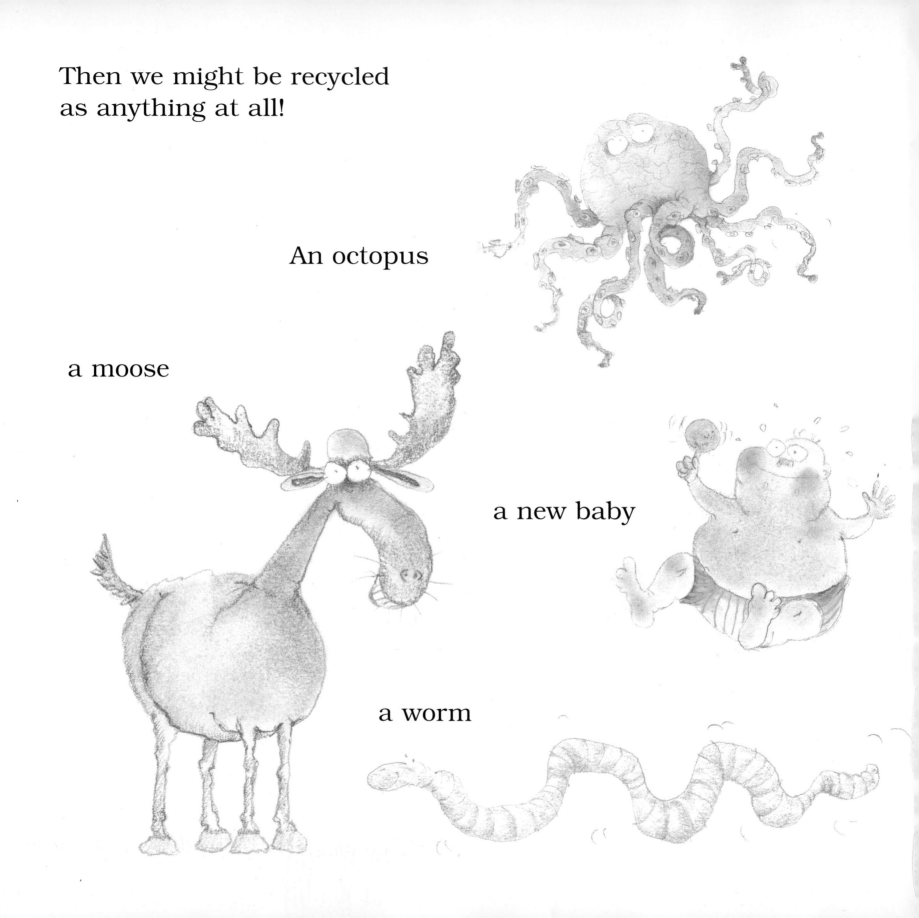

a sheep

a ghost

a pickled onion

PICKL

an alien

or even
two
scrawny
chickens.

What would you like us to be?

THIS IS A BORZOI BOOK PUBLISHED BY ALFRED A. KNOPF, INC.
Copyright © 1996 by Babette Cole
All rights reserved under International and Pan-American Copyright Conventions. Published in the
United States by Alfred A. Knopf, Inc., New York, and simultaneously in Canada by Random House of Canada Limited,
Toronto. Distributed by Random House, Inc., New York. Originally published in
Great Britain in 1996 by Jonathan Cape Limited, Random House UK Limited.

http://www.randomhouse.com/

First American edition: 1997

Library of Congress Cataloging-in-Publication Data
Cole, Babette.
Drop dead / written and illustrated by Babette Cole.
p. cm.
Summary: A rather eccentric Gran and Granddad retell their dangerous life stories and
speculate about what may become of them after they drop down dead.
ISBN: 0-679-88358-4 (trade)
[1. Grandparents—Fiction. 2. Death—Fiction. 3. Reincarnation—Fiction.] I. Title.
PZ7.C6734Dr   1996
[Fic]—dc20
96-16934

Printed in Italy

10 9 8 7 6 5 4 3 2 1